ELLEN RASKIN

SPECTACLES

ALADDIN BOOKS
MACMILLAN PUBLISHING COMPANY   NEW YORK

Text and illustrations copyright © 1968 by Ellen Raskin

Macmillan Publishing Company
866 Third Avenue, New York, NY 10022
Collier Macmillan Canada, Inc.

First Aladdin Edition 1972
Second Aladdin Books edition 1988

Printed in U.S.A.

10 9 8 7 6 5 4 3 2 1

Raskin, Ellen.
    Spectacles/by Ellen Raskin.
        p.   cm.
    Summary : A nearsighted little girl talks about and shows some of
the unusual things she saw before being fitted with glasses.
    ISBN 0-689-71271-5
    [1. Eye—Diseases and defects—Fiction. 2. Eyeglasses—Fiction.]
I. Title.
PZ7.R1817Sp 1988
[E]—dc19   88-10363   CIP AC

This book is dedicated to
Lila, Melvin, and me,
and to all boys and girls who wear glasses,
either some of the time or all of the time.
(Sunglasses don't count.)

My name is Iris Fogel and I didn't always wear glasses.

Not until a fire-breathing dragon knocked at our door.

It was Great-aunt Fanny.

The giant pygmy nuthatch on our front lawn was only

my good friend Chester.

"Come and watch my Indian make funny faces," I said.

"Those are cowboys, silly," said my good friend Chester.

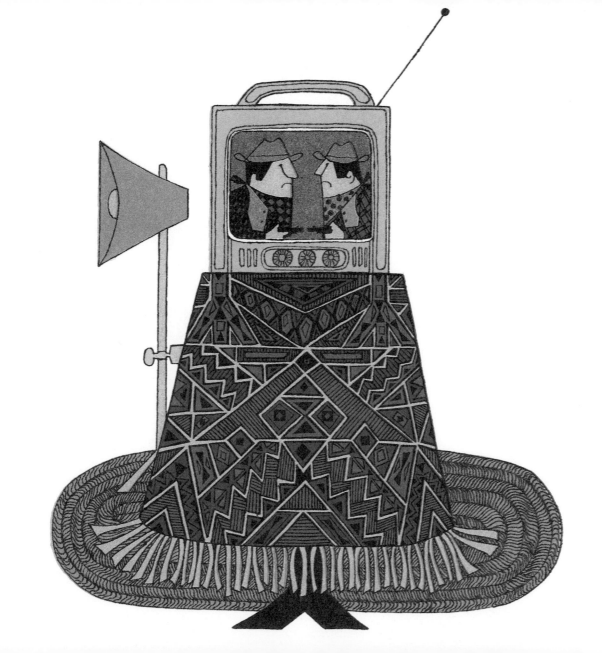

My mother insisted that the chestnut mare in the parlor

was my baby-sitter,

that Mrs. Schmidlapp's big friendly looking bull dog

was a little kitten,

and that it certainly was not polite to call Chester

a fat kangaroo.

Things grew worse when I saw a fuzzy green caterpillar.

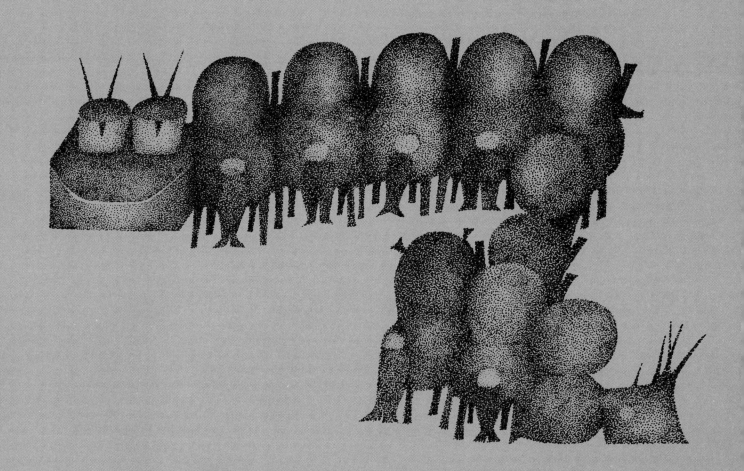

"Where?" the teacher shrieked.

That's when Mother took me to a blue elephant, who said:

"Iris needs glasses!"

"No," I cried.

"You will see much better."

"No," I sobbed.

"You can have contact lenses
when you are older."

"No," I bawled.

"Even some presidents of the
United States wore glasses."

"No," I screamed.

So the doctor prescribed glasses
and mother took me to

the optician, who said:
"Would you like round,
oval, square, oblong
or harlequin frames?"
"No!"
"Thick, thin or medium frames,
red, white, blue, green,
black, brown or tortoiseshell?"
"No!"
"Scotch plaid, pin-striped,
checkerboard or polka dot?"
"No!"

"Would you like to look
younger or older,
sweeter or smarter,
like a scholar or a movie star?"
"Like a movie star," I said.
Mother couldn't decide between
frames that made me
look adorable and frames that
made me look intelligent.
She chose the intelligent ones
because of the scare
I gave my teacher.

A few days later I got my glasses

with glass in them.

No one seemed to notice,

except Chester,

who said I looked different.

"You look pretty different yourself,

Chester," I replied.

Now my problems are over.

Even Great-aunt Fanny thinks

I am well-behaved.

You see, everything looks like

I suppose it's supposed to look,

except for that red rhinoceros with a tulip in its ear.